FrankinSchool

To Fredrik, again
Thanks for helping me kick off this adventure.
Excited for all your adventures that lie ahead.

Also by Caryn Rivadeneira
Frankinschool Mystery #1: Monster Match
Frankinschool Mystery #2: The Cupsnake Escape
Frankinschool Mystery #3: Gone to the Dogs!
Helper Hounds: Penny Helps Portia Face Her Fears
Helper Hounds: Sparky Helps Mary Make New Friends
Helper Hounds: Noodle Helps Gabriel Say Goodbye
Helper Hounds: Robot Helps Max and Lily Deal with Bullies
Helper Hounds: King Tut Helps Ming Stay Weird
Helper Hounds: Spooky Helps Danny Tell the Truth
Helper Hounds: Brisket Helps Miryam with Online Learning
Helper Hounds: Louis Helps Ajani Fight Racism
Edward and Annie: A Penguin Adventure
Gritty and Graceful: 15 Inspiring Women of the Bible
Grit and Grace: Heroic Women of the Bible

FrankinSchool
The What-If Winter Wonderfest

by Caryn Rivadeneira
illustrated by Dani Jones

Egremont, Massachusetts

RED CHAIR PRESS
BOOKS FOR YOUNG READERS

www.redchairpress.com

Free Discussion Guide Available online

Publisher's Cataloging-In-Publication Data
(Provided by Cassidy Cataloging Services, Inc.)

Names: Rivadeneira, Caryn Dahlstrand, author. | Jones, Dani, 1983- illustrator.

Title: Frankinschool. 4, The What-If Winter Wonderfest / by Caryn Rivadeneira ; illustrated by Dani Jones.

Other Titles: What-If Winter Wonderfest

Description: Egremont, Massachusetts : Red Chair Press, [2025] | Series: Frankinschool mysteries | Interest age level: 007-010. | Summary: Fred, Luisa, and Drake are tasked with writing the school Winter Pageant. With Luisa's Broadway-famous uncle directing, they create the What-If Winter Wonderfest, unleashing a whirlwind of spooky, festive chaos and humorous discovery.-- Publisher.

Identifiers: ISBN: 978-1-64371-406-6 (hardcover) | 978-1-64371-408-0 (ePub3 S/L multiuser) | 978-1-64371-407-3 (multiuser ebook PDF) | 978-1-64371-409-7 (ePub3 TR) | 978-1-64371-410-3 (Kf8 ebook) | 978-1-64371-411-0 (audiobook) | LCCN: 2024947210

Subjects: LCSH: Pageants--Juvenile fiction. | Monsters--Juvenile fiction. | Creative writing--Juvenile fiction. | Theatrical producers and directors--Juvenile fiction. | Friendship--Juvenile fiction. | CYAC: Pageants--Fiction. | Monsters--Fiction. | Creative writing--Fiction. | Producers and directors--Fiction. | Friendship--Fiction. | LCGFT: Monster fiction. | BISAC: JUVENILE FICTION / Performing Arts / Theater & Musicals. | JUVENILE FICTION / Monsters. | JUVENILE FICTION / Social Themes / Friendship.

Classification: LCC: PZ7.1.R57627 Frw 2025 | DDC: [Fic]--dc23
LC record available at https://lccn.loc.gov/2022950228

Main body text set in Amasis Regular 17/27
Text copyright © Caryn Rivadeneira

Copyright © 2026 Red Chair Press LLC

RED CHAIR PRESS, the RED CHAIR and associated logos are registered trademarks of Red Chair Press LLC.

All rights reserved. No part of this book may be reproduced, stored in an information or retrieval system, or transmitted in any form by any means, electronic, mechanical including photocopying, recording, or otherwise without the prior written permission from the Publisher. For permissions, contact info@redchairpress.com

Printed in Canada

0525 1P F25FRN

TABLE OF CONTENTS

CHAPTER 1:
Losing His Touch................1

CHAPTER 2:
Smells and Bells 13

CHAPTER 3:
Write What Brings You Joy..........27

CHAPTER 4:
A Poet and Didn't Know It! 37

CHAPTER 5:
Going Up?......................53

CHAPTER 6:
The Attic 67

CHAPTER 7:
The Worst Rear-end Ever! 77

CHAPTER 8:
What Are You Afraid Of?..........91

CHAPTER 1:
LOSING HIS TOUCH

Fred inhaled. Most kids hated the way their gym smelled. But Fred liked it. Not the stale sweat and stinky gym shoes so much. But just before lunch time, when the kitchen behind the gym got too warm and the staff opened the side doors, the gym smelled like a mix of tater tots and fresh, crisp air. Plus, basketballs. The gym always smelled like basketballs. Even up here on the stage.

"Ugh," Luisa said, plugging her nose. "I hope they spray some air freshener before my uncle gets here."

"I hope we get some good ideas before your uncle gets here," Drake said.

"Well, if you wouldn't keep insisting that we have to bring *Krampus*[*] into a Christmas pageant maybe we could get somewhere!" Luisa said.

"And if you could stop insisting that we had to include the three wise camels or whatever they are maybe we'd have at least one decent idea," Drake snapped back.

"That's the thing!" the girl across the table said. "You're too stuck on Christmas. My family celebrates Hanukkah and Kwanzaa and—" she pointed to the boy sitting next

[*]Krampus is a half-goat monster from myths who punishes naughty children.

to her "—his family celebrates Diwali. We should celebrate all the holidays that celebrate light in the darkness. Not everyone believes in Santa or Christmas, you know."

Fred closed his eyes and breathed in again. Maybe it didn't smell that great after all. But at least it distracted him from the bickering happening at his table. Fred, Luisa, Drake and two third graders had been chosen to help write the Winter Wonder Fest school pageant. Luisa's uncle, the world-famous Broadway director Juan Pierre Reyes, was coming in all the way from New York City to help them write it.

For the life of him, Fred couldn't imagine why someone as famous as *the* Juan Pierre Reyes—as Luisa insisted on calling him—

would come all this way just to help with a dumb elementary school play. I mean, *the* Juan Pierre Reyes could be making a lot of money directing famous actors in New York City. Once, Luisa told Fred, her uncle even won a huge award for some show about dogs. Or was it cats? Fred couldn't remember. Luisa said her uncle was coming out because he loved her and was always willing to help. But Fred wasn't so sure. Something about it seemed weird.

Either way. *The* Juan Pierre Reyes was coming to their school to help them write and direct *their* holiday pageant. All they needed was an idea. One good idea. Which they didn't have.

As the arguing continued—and

escalated—Fred straightened up in his chair and said, "Can we just do something peaceful—like, everyone stands around, holding hands and singing or whatever?"

"I am not holding your hand!" Luisa snapped. "That's the dumbest idea ever."

Fred rolled his eyes and said, "I wish we could just each be writing poems. I like poems. Then it's just me and my own thoughts. No 'dialogue.' No stage directions. No worrying about what you or some *director* is going to say about it."

"Some director?" Luisa said. "My uncle is—"

"We know. We know," Drake said. *"The* Juan Pierre Reyes. Coming all the way from New York City."

The boy and girl across the table snickered. Luisa shot them a glance, and their mouths tightened.

"Yes," Luisa said. "And he is nice and brilliant and funny and a true *artiste!* He's the best—and it's amazing that he agreed to help us."

Drake flipped open his notebook. He shook his head as he looked at the blank page. "Well, since all we've come up with is a bunch of kids holding hands singing about peace, I don't think this artiste is going to have much to help us with…"

Luisa rolled her eyes.

The other kids at the table laughed.

"Maybe we should have our holiday play be about arguing—that's what everyone does at holidays, right?" Fred said. "Everybody gathers around a table to eat and fight about who is right. Who is wrong. What ideas are good and what ideas are the 'dumbest ever.' Just like this conversation."

"Peace does seem like a pretty good idea," the boy across the table said with a shrug of his shoulders.

But before they could brainstorm any other ideas, Ms. Martinez—the teacher in charge of this school project—stomped up the stairs leading onto the stage.

"All right, all right," Ms. Martinez announced. "Our director, Mr. Juan Pierre Reyes—"

Fred, Drake, and Luisa smiled as Ms. Martinez fanned herself.

"—will be here any minute now. He'll help us develop and write our program, but we do need to have a solid idea for him to develop! I hope you've all be gathering lots of great ideas for Winter Wonder Fest!"

Fred grabbed his Idea Notebook out of his backpack. This was full of ideas. At least for mysteries, for short stories, for his favorite: poems. He even had an idea of a story for the school newspaper. Fred looked at the brochure from a haunted hotel his family had stayed at that summer. He'd tucked it into his Idea Notebook thinking the spookiest place students had ever visited would make a fun story. But the newspaper teacher had said no. Newspapers were about *true* stories. Not *ghost* stories. Fred smiled again about

ghost stories not being true.

But it didn't matter now. Fred had come up with nothing for the Winter Wonder Fest—except peaceful kids holding hands.

Fred hated to admit that Luisa was right. But it was a pretty dumb idea.

How could he write a poem about almost anything and not be able to come up with an idea for a holiday play? His poems had introduced them to their friend Frank the ghost, transformed them into Frankinschool, Princesa Luisa, and the snake-headed Snake-ula. His poems had sent them on adventures that Fred still had trouble believing ever really happened. Maybe the newspaper teacher was right.

Especially since they hadn't seen Frank or Jeremiah the ghosts in months now. They'd all tried writing *What If* poems to see if it would bring Frank and his friends back, if it would open the doors for more mysterious adventures.

But nothing happened.

Not anymore.

No matter how hard they tried, that spooky green mist that once put students and teachers to sleep failed to materialize. No matter what they tried, no secret rooms or ghost friends emerged. No matter what they wrote, they stayed their same old selves—Fred, Luisa, and Drake.

To make matters worse, the last time they did transform, Luisa wrote the poem! It was her magic that had worked. Not Fred's.

Fred sighed.

No good ideas.

No magic poems.

Maybe Fred had lost his touch.

CHAPTER TWO
SMELLS AND BELLS

The smell of something spicy—churchy, even—wafted up to the stage. Fred took another sniff and thought again about the mingling of smells. Then he looked around at the stage. He'd been up here a million times since his very first day of kindergarten. He'd stood on, sat on, and even—ugh— danced across this stage during assemblies, awards ceremonies, class plays, and the music-class programs. What a weird mix of things happened on this stage. What a weird mix of things happened in this whole space! Who mixes a stage with a gym with a cafeteria? Gross.

But Ms. Martinez had suggested they use the stage for inspiration. After all, they were writing a play—and plays are performed on stages.

"Let the stage *speak* to you," Ms. Martinez had said. "Let the wisdom of the playwrights whose words have been recited in this space inspire you."

Fred looked around—at the heavy gray curtain hanging askew on one end. At the tight ropes used to open and close it—at least, that's what Fred assumed they were for. At the yellowing door that led down to the kitchen. At the cement-block wall along the back. And at the—the wait! What was *that*?

Never in Fred's years at this school and millions of times up on this stage had he noticed the slim brass and glass chute that ran along the wall at the back of the stage.

Fred squinted and craned his neck up to where it disappeared into the ceiling. Then he looked down where it sunk below the floor. It looked like an old-timey mail chute like he'd seen in the haunted hotel. Incidentally, that hotel had a stage too. But that stage—unlike this one—was inspiring. With its ornate carpeted steps, cream and gold columns, and the thickly curtained windows that curved along the back.

That mail chute belonged in a hotel like that. Not on a school stage. Where would that mail chute even go? There was nothing above or below it!

Or was there?

A fresh waft of tater tots-basketballs-and-fresh air brought Fred back to reality. The reality of an old mail chute at the back of a stage in a gym surrounded by the smells of basketballs, tater tots, crisp air, and now, spices?

Weird mixes all around, Fred thought. *Wait a minute...*

"Why is your uncle's name Juan *Pierre*?" Fred asked.

"Why's your name *Fred*?" Luisa asked back with a roll of her eyes.

"I mean: it's a weird mix of Spanish and French, right?"

Luisa shrugged. "I wouldn't say *weird*. When my *abuela* found out one of her ancestors was from France, she wanted to honor that. So, instead of Juan Pedro, they went with Juan *Pierre*. It works for him."

Fred nodded. "It does. Like the mix of smells work for the gym—"

Luisa pulled her nose up and shook her head. "Definitely *not* like that!"

Drake plugged his nose and agreed.

"I'm saying, like the mix of names works for your uncle and the mix of smells does work for the gym, I wonder if the mix of holidays could work for our pageant," Fred said.

"Like *what if* we mixed all the different ways people celebrate this time of year?" Drake said.

"Exactly," Fred said. "Do you think we could do it without arguing? Like, maybe we could find out what we have in common? My parents always tell us to look for that—rather than looking for differences."

"Okay," Luisa said. "How about we all go around and name what and how we celebrate—and think of ways our friends and neighbors do, too."

As the kids around the table shared the holidays and ways they celebrated, Fred wrote down the themes:

- Lighting candles for the menorah during Hanukkah
- Lighting candles for the crown at St. Lucia
- Lighting the candles for Advent and Christmas Eve
- Lighting the candles for Kwanzaa

- Lighting the oil lamps for Diwali
- Lighting bonfires and yule logs for solstice celebrations

"And we celebrate *Día de los Reyes*," Luisa said. "The day the three wise men—though, since it's me and my moms at home, we say three wise *women*—visit the baby Jesus. We leave out hay and carrots for the camels and put out our shoes so the wise women leave us candy."

"That sounds nice," Drake said.

Frank nodded. It was nice—but something was missing.

"Do you burn anything?" Fred asked.

"Sometimes my mom lights a frankincense stick," Luisa said. "You know, because the three wise men brought gold, frankincense, and myrrh? But it doesn't glow. Just smells."

Fred sighed. They were *almost* onto something.

"So, we don't all light up things," Fred said. "What else do these traditions have in common?"

"It's kind of creepy sometimes," the girl across the table offered. "All the lights—in the dark."

The boy next to her shivered. "Yeah, the way they cast shadows."

"The frankincense releases a spooky string of smoke," Luisa said. "Looks like a spirit wafting up."

"One year, my gran told us about

Krampus," Drake said. "We don't celebrate that. But it sounded scary—a horned-monster guy chases naughty kids through the streets!"

"My neighbors celebrate the solstice," the girl said. "They invite us over to tell ghost stories around the bonfire. Then someone rings a bell. It's *fun*—but so creepy in the dark."

"Hmmmmm," Fred said, writing down the ideas. "We always go into the city to see *A Christmas Carol*. You know, Scrooge, Bah Humbug, the Ghost of Christmas past…"

What if…? Fred thought as he began to scribble.

What if this season is not about light?

What if it's about embracing the night?
Because these spooky stories help us be brave.
These shadows and ghosts help us behave.
Because what scares us connects us
What scares us compels us
What scares us...

Fred stopped. He'd been scared plenty of times in the past year or so. First, when his poem about being Frank-in-school turned him *into* Frankinschool. Then when his next what-if poem turned cupcakes into cupsnakes and he, Drake, and Luisa had to save the local high school. And then, last time he tried this, his what-if poem *failed*. Nothing happened. Until Luisa disappeared and a secret panel door in the library opened up and they met Frank the ghost's terrifying ghost friend—and, well, now the library was also a humane society.

Long story, Fred thought. But he wasn't exactly sure what being scared could do. Except make you brave. Except make you better. Except make you kinder and more understanding.

And that's what these holidays were all about, right? That's what they all had in common. Peace and love and hope and joy and all that.

All these traditions centered around flickering lights in cold dark nights, visits from mythical or magical creatures and important people. All these traditions and recipes and songs and stories were all—in their own way—ghosts of holidays past.

"I got it!" Fred said a little too loudly.

But his idea would have to wait.

Because *the* Juan Pierre Reyes had just stepped onto the stage with a dramatic flip of his scarf.

CHAPTER THREE
WRITE WHAT BRINGS YOU JOY

"**T**io Juan!" Luisa yelled, her chair screeching as she pushed up from it.

"*Mi amor*!" Juan Pierre said, hugging her tightly.

When Luisa released her grip, *the* Juan Pierre Reyes adjusted his jacket and held out his hands toward Ms. Martinez.

"You must be the amazing Ms. Martinez," Juan Pierre said. "My niece has told me so much about you."

Fred, Luisa, and Drake smiled at one another as Ms. Martinez's cheeks turned fire red.

"And, of course," Ms. Martinez said, "Luisa has nothing but the best words about you! We are so honored to have you join us and help us with your play. I just wish—"And here, Ms. Martinez gave a tight, worried smile to the table of writers "—we were further along in our idea process. I'm afraid the students haven't landed on anything they love yet."

"Ah," Juan Pierre said, "great ideas take time. They take time! And good theater cannot be rushed—except when the audience is already seated!"

Fred wasn't sure what was so funny, but

as Juan Pierre, Ms. Martinez, and Luisa laughed, he let out a couple chuckles.

"We do have one idea," Luisa said. "Imagine this—" And here Luisa took on a tone that Fred had never heard. She fanned her fingers and held both hands in front of her face. Her eyes wide and voice deep. "Children from all over the world—different countries, different cultures—sing about the traditions we have in common."

Juan Pierre stroked his chin.

"Good, good..." he said, nodding his head toward the other children at the table. "Who else?"

The stage was silent. The only noise was the clanking of kitchen gear from the lunch staff.

Fred cleared this throat.

Juan Pierre's head turned immediately in his direction. "Yes?" he asked.

"Um…" Fred said. "What if…"

"Oh, here we go again with the what-ifs!" Luisa whispered. "You *know* the what-ifs don't work anymore Fred!"

Juan Pierre snapped his fingers in his niece's direction. "Let him finish," he said, rolling his hands in front of him. "What if…"

"What if," Fred said more confidently this time. "We told a ghost story. Every tradition we talked about actually sounds a little spooky at times. Flickering candles. Long shadows. Stories in the dark. Creepy creatures. Ghosts of Christmas past. That's part of the *wonder* of this season too."

Juan Pierre nodded and stroked his chin. "Yes, yes," he said. "I like that. One way people have dealt with the darkening of Winter's days has been to light candles and brighten the darkness, certainly, but

it's also why people choose to confront it, confound it—" and here Juan Pierre paused dramatically as he scanned the table of children, who each watched him with eyes wide and mouths open "—and *combat* it with spooky stories of their own. This time of year heightens our curiosity, makes us wonder what lurks in the looming darkness, gives us chills—literally and figuratively…"

Here, Ms. Martinez giggled nervously and said, "Wow. I love your creative mind. But I'm not sure a ghost story is going to work for our families. Little kids come to see this play."

Juan Pierre nodded again and said, "No, no. You're right of course. Too scary. The Winter Wonder Fest should be happy.

A celebration of joyful things we have in common. Let's see where that takes us."

Juan Pierre clapped twice and said, "Let's take fifteen minutes to each come up with our own joy-filled story lines—from across cultures and traditions. Practice writing them in the script-style Ms. Martinez told you about. Each of us can come up with our own scenes. We can see how to piece them together. This is called the 'pearl necklace method' in writing."

Fred sighed and picked up his pen. Fred had been convinced his was a good one— *the* Juan Pierre Reyes had liked it after all. But surprise, surprise: another dumb idea.

Luisa rubbed her hands together before snatching up her pen. "I love the idea of a joyous journey through the winter solstice ending with a visit from the three wise women and their camels!"

"And I might find a way to bring a happy Krampus into this," Drake said. "I like that dude. He can light the candles rather than torture the kids."

"I like that, I guess," Fred said with a defeated smile.

Drake looked at Fred and said, "Sorry Ms. Martinez shot down your idea. It was good. We might like scary. But not everybody does. Write what brings you joy."

"That's great advice from your friend," Juan Pierre said. "Write whatever brings you joy."

And as Fred looked up at *the* Juan Pierre Reyes, Fred could've sworn he saw him wink.

CHAPTER FOUR
A POET AND DIDN'T KNOW IT!

Fred's pen flew across his paper, scratching out lines as fast as he could get them down.

> What if writing ghost stories brings me joy?
> What if shadows and secrets feel like toys?
> What if the best part of the winter
> Isn't the fests but the wonder…

Wait. This was supposed to be a play. Not a poem.

Fred began to scratch out what he'd written.

Then he stopped. Because something at the back of the stage caught his eye.

Zip.

Something had gone down the brass mail chute. Fred was sure of it. Once again, he tried to puzzle out what could be above the stage. The outside of the gym had nothing above it. He knew because he, Drake, and Luisa had spent many recesses trying to hit wiffle balls onto the roof. Once, one made it. Fred said it was because of his great pitch. Luisa said it was because of her great hit. Drake said it was because of the wind.

Flash.

There it was again.

Was that a piece of notebook paper going down the chute?

This time, even Juan Pierre seemed to notice. Though no one else did.

"Nine minutes until we share ideas," Ms. Martinez said with a syncopated clap. "Let's get writing."

So, Fred turned back to his writing and tried again. This time written as a play.

Scene 1

Old-fashioned stage in haunted hotel. The theater and stage are dark. Ghosts and ghouls dressed up as holiday characters move about the stage as a narrator tells the story.

NARRATOR

We turn on the lights to cover our fear.

But what if it's the darkness we should draw near?

What if the quiet and stillness could bring us cheer?

What if that's what we all celebrated this time of year?

What if rather than presents and candles and parties

We all took a turn telling ghost stories?

Of caroling ghouls and gift-bearing monsters

Of three wise women atop camels and... lobsters?

Fred smiled to himself. He'd work on that later.

NARRATOR

Because fear's what we share, what we have in common.

Whether we eat turkey or latkes or... ramen.

What if we talked about the things that made us shiver?

What if telling ghost stories helped us deliver—

Helped us deliver...

Helped us deliver...

Fred still wasn't quite sure what these ghost stories were supposed to deliver. And as he continued to wonder—

GACHUNK.

Gasps rose from the writing table as the lights all around them—on the stage, in the gym, even in the kitchen—shut off. Loudly.

"Nobody move," Ms. Martinez said. "I'll find the— Wait. What is that sm...?"

In the darkness, Fred heard Ms. Martinez softly slumping to the ground, followed by the two bonks of the boy and girl across the table as their heads landed on the table. All followed by that same spooky, churchy smell. This time, much stronger.

"It's frankincense, " Luisa said. "That's what my moms burn on Día de los Reyes."

Then Fred heard a familiar jingle of diamonds, followed by a hiss of snakes.

Fred reached for his neck. Two knobs jutted out. He lifted his feet, now heavy from boots.

It was happening. Fred was once

again Frank in school. Frank-in-school. Frankinschool.

As the lights ga-cluncked back on, a light green mist rolled across the floor.

Frankinschool smiled sheepishly at Snake-ula and Princesa Luisa before noticing the stage all around them. No longer

was it the bland gray cement of the school stage. No longer was it even connected to their school gym. No longer did it smell like tater tots and basketballs and crisp air. No longer could they hear the lunchroom staff clanking pots in the kitchen.

Now they were on a stage—on *that* stage—from the haunted hotel. Cream and gold-colored columns rose around them. Ornate burgundy carpet stretched beneath them. Behind them, thickly curtained windows bowed out. And yet, there was that mail chute still there.

"What did you write?" Princesa asked.

"Nothing!" Frankinschool said. "Just an idea for an opening for a play about holiday ghost stories! I promise. Besides, my what-if poems haven't worked in forever. I should ask you what *you* wrote!"

"I had an idea for a baking show play where students made their families' best traditional desserts," Princesa said.

"Another *baking* competition is the last

thing we need," Snake-ula said as the snakes on his head wove themselves into a cake shape.

Frankinschool and Princesa looked at Snake-ula. Frankinschool had forgotten how strange his Medusa-like monster was.

"Good point," Princesa said.

"But I was just *thinking* about a stage like this from a hotel we stayed at. Look," Frankinschool said, reaching for the hotel brochure. "It's not here!"

"You must've written something," Princesa said. "Let me see your Idea Notebook."

Princesa's arm lurched toward Frankinschool.

"Let me see it!" Princesa said again,

snappier this time.

Frankinschool grabbed for his notebook, intending to hold it high away from Luisa's prying eyes. But it was gone too.

"Where's my notebook?" Frankinschool nearly shouted. "You took it!"

"Did not!" Princesa said. "Why would I ask for it if I already had it?"

The girl across the table adjusted her sleepy position at the table. Ms. Martinez let out a loud snore from her slumped position in the corner.

"Guys," Snake-ula said. "Haven't we learned anything? Getting *angry* isn't going to help. If you didn't write a poem and you didn't write a poem…"

"Did *you* write a poem?" Frankinschool asked.

"No," Snake-ula said. "I don't know how to write poems. I just wrote this."

Snake-ula held up his paper. The head

snakes dived for it. He pulled the paper further in front of him. It read:

> WHAT IF FRANK AND JEREMIAH THE GHOSTS SHOWED UP AND DID THE PLAY FOR US SO WE'D STOP ARGUING ABOUT WHOSE IDEA WAS BEST.

"So it *was* you," Frankinschool said.

Snake-ula suddenly beamed. "I guess it was me! I'm a poet and I didn't even know it. A magician, you might say—"

"Yeah, but if it was you," Princesa said. "Then where are they? Where are Frank and Jeremiah? And wait—" Princesa gasped. "Where's my uncle?"

Just then, another piece of paper dropped down the mail chute.

CHAPTER FIVE
GOING UP?

Frankinschool, Princesa, and Snake-ula shot up from their chairs. Frankinschool nearly tumbled forward. He'd forgotten how heavy his frankenfeet were in those boots. Princesa galloped around the stage. She peered behind curtains and ducked behind columns.

Frankinschool stomped toward the mail chute. "I don't know where your uncle went, but something tells me finding out where this tube goes will help," Frankinschool said.

"There's nothing above the stage," Snake-ula said. "I don't think there's anything below it either. Just that creepy storage space where they keep the goals and the parachutes and the—" Snake-ula shuddered "—the ropes."

"But we're not in the gym anymore. We're not on *that* stage, are we?" Princesa said as they took in the elegant ballroom that now protruded from the front of their stage.

"No," Frankinschool said. "It's *just* like that hotel my family stayed in last summer. I mean, it's like we were transported there. I don't understand!"

"So," Snake-ula said, pointing to a set

of doors on the side of the ballroom. "Will it still be our school out there? If we go through those doors?"

The snakes helicoptered above Snake-ula's head as he jumped off the stage onto the ballroom floor.

Frankinschool shrugged. "Dunno," he said.

"Because if this whole place has turned into that hotel, then there's probably something on top of this stage—and below it," Snake-ula said. "Somebody—or some*thing*—could be using that chute."

Frankinschool nodded. He'd explored every inch of that hotel when they'd stayed overnight on their way to his cousin's house. He'd snuck into second-floor ballrooms and meeting rooms—that's how he found the stage in the first place. He'd wandered through long, twisting hallways and discovered secret elevators. He'd taken back staircases and somehow ended up in a tangle of bed sheets and towels in the laundry room.

Oops! A housekeeper had escorted him out.

But Frankinschool could not remember anything being *above* that ballroom. Part of the lobby was below it—that he remembered. He had sat on the lobby's shabby floral sofas and looked up at the balconies that framed a stained-glass skylight two stories above. Wedding guests had milled around those balconies, sipping drinks and munching on tiny somethings before heading into the ballroom beyond it. Frankinschool—Fred then, he supposed—had squinted into the bright light that streamed through the skylight trying to figure out what they were eating.

Wait, Frankinschool thought. *That wedding was at nighttime.*

Frankinschool had assumed the light coming through the ceiling was the sun. But it had to be a fake light. So that means something could be above the ballroom. But what? Hotel rooms? An attic?

They would just have to find out. Frankinschool looked at the doors on the three sides of the ballrooms. Of course, it would all depend on what was beyond these doors. And which door they chose. Would it be their school, or would it be the hotel or would it be something else entirely?

"Which way should we go?" Frankinschool asked his friends.

"This way," they each said pointing in a different direction.

"Before we start arguing again, because this is like the hotel I stayed at," Frankinschool said. "I think we should go through these doors. There should be a hallway and a stairwell just out here."

Frankinschool motioned to his friends, and together they pushed open the doors and stepped into yet another unknown.

• • •

It was a hallway. Not the same hallway as

the hotel where Frankinschool had stayed. But definitely a hotel hallway. And an old one. With worn patterned carpet and a musty odor.

"Ugh," Princesa said, plugging her nose. "What is it with these *smells* today?"

"I dunno," Frankinschool said. "I'm more worried about *those*."

Frankinschool pointed to the multi-colored candles mounted on the walls that hung between the numbered doors. Their flames roared high and cast long shadows across the dark hallways.

Between them, green garland, silver tinsel, and ribbons in gold, red, green, and black trimmed the hallways and seemed to tease the flames.

"Seem like kind of a safety hazard," Snake-ula said as the snakes darted toward the flames. "All this stuff just waiting to catch fire. And geez—you walk out of your room and—BAM—into a flame."

"It's like we're in an old *castle* or something," Princesa said. "Which I like, of course, but this is weird. What are all these

decorations for?"

Frankinschool began to count the candles. "Seven. Five. Nine. One," he said. "Kwanzaa. Advent. Hanukkah. Solstice. And the ribbons—the colors. The same?"

"What do you mean?" Princesa asked. "Like the mix of holidays?"

But before Frankinschool could answer,

the snakes pointed ahead, their forked tongues flicking as a familiar smell surrounded them.

"Frankincense, again," Princesa said. Then she smiled. "Frankinschool's Frankincense. You should start a business."

"Ha, ha," Frankinschool said. "Very funny. Let's figure out where this smell is coming from first."

"Look," Snake-ula said. "Stairs!"

And sure enough: Just up ahead was an EXIT sign above a door marked with an etching of steps.

"Perfect!" Frankinschool said. "We need to see where that mail chute comes from and—and who is sending stuff through it. That'll be the clue to finding where your uncle is. I just know it!"

Frankinschool grabbed the handle to the door and pushed. The strong scent of frankincense overwhelmed them. They plugged their noses and stepped into the stairwell.

Frankinschool didn't know what he was expecting, but it wasn't this. In front of them a wrought-iron railing and stairs twisted up and spiraled down toward who knew what.

"Cool!" Snake-ula said, pushing ahead and starting to stomp up. "I love spiral staircases!"

"Wait," Princesa said. "Why are we going up first? I think we should go down."

"We gotta go *up* to see who or what is sending stuff through that chute,"

Frankinschool said.

"We should go *down* to see where the stuff is going," Princesa said, her voice rising. "Who cares where it *starts*?"

"I do!" Snake-ula said. "I say we go up!"

As the arguing between his friends continued, Frankinschool put a frankenfinger to his lips as the sound of a muddled, out-of-tune holiday song spilled into the stairwell from somewhere *above* them.

"Listen," he said.

"Sounds like, 'Walking in a Winter Wonderland,' but weirder," Snake-ula said.

"Creepier," Princesa said. "Like it's being played on one of those old-timey phonographs we saw at the history museum."

"I think we have to see what's up there," Frankinschool said as he set one frankenboot on the step and then the next. He looked at Princesa who nodded and joined him on the steps. Then he looked up and grabbed tight to the railing, which wobbled a little under his tight grip.

Princesa and Snake-ula followed him as they twisted and turned until the stairs stopped—opening into yet another attic.

CHAPTER SIX
THE ATTIC

The attic was bare. Totally empty. Except for the mail chute, which ran along the back wall, and a small table that held a record player. On it, a record wobbled and wobbled and played—as Snake-ula said—a warped version of "Walking in a Winter Wonderland." Beside it, lay a notebook and the hotel brochure.

"Hey!" Frankinschool said, rushing forward. "That's my notebook!"

Frankinschool flipped through it. Several pages had been torn out.

"How did it get here?" Frankinschool asked.

"Look!" Snake-ula said. "A trap door!"

Sure enough, across from where the warbly record wobbled, a tiny handle and hinges rose from the wooden floor planks.

"Should I open it?" Snake-ula said, kneeling in front of the square door. The snakes had already wrapped themselves around the handle.

"Sure," Frankinschool said, clomping back toward it.

Snake-ula shooed the snakes out of the way and tugged. The door opened without even a creak. No dust flew from its sides.

"It's been used recently," Princesa said as they all leaned over to see where the trap door led.

Beneath it ran a length of metal grating with bars along the side. Beneath *that* was the stage they had been on and the table where they had been sitting.

"It's a catwalk," Princesa said. "My uncle took me up on one once."

"How did we not notice this when we were sitting right under it?" Snake-ula asked.

Frankinschool shrugged. "We didn't look up," he said. "In fairness, there was a lot going on."

"Look!" Princesa said. "A fishing pole."

"So that's how they got my notebook!" Frankinschool said. "When the lights went out, someone must've fished it right up. They must've sent the pages from my notebook down the mail chute. But who?"

After a pause, the three of them looked at each other and said: "Frank."

"But why?' Snake-ula asked.

"We know he likes to steal my stuff!" Frankinschool said. "He never has great ideas of his own. He told us that—that's why he relies on us for our poems. But why does Frank want my ideas for a Christmas pageant?"

"A *winter* pageant," Princesa and Snake-ula said together.

"Fine. A winter pageant," Frankinschool said. "Either way, it doesn't make any sense. What do ghosts care about school plays?"

"Hold on," Princesa said. "Remember how excited my *tio* got about your ghost story idea?"

Frankinschool nodded.

"What if this isn't Frank doing this at all? What if it's my tio!"

"But your uncle was on the stage with us until the lights went out," Snake-ula said. "He couldn't have stolen the notebook and gotten up the stairs and sent the pages down to who-knows-where. There wasn't time. Besides, why would he send them down the chute? Why not just hold on to them?"

Snake-ula had a point, Frankinschool thought.

"What if Frank's got my tio?" Princesa said with a gasp. "He would've heard *the world-famous* Juan Pierre Reyes was coming to our school and nabbed him for—ahh!—ransom." Princesa's diamond bracelets clinked as she brought a gloved hand to her face and drew out the word.

"Frank wouldn't do that," Frankinschool said. "He's a *ghost*. He's not a *monster*—no offense, Snake-ula. Besides, how does a ghost capture a person? Impossible. I think you were right the first time. Did you ever tell your uncle about our adventures with Frank?"

Princesa nodded. "Last time we visited him—when we were up on that catwalk. My tio told me how lots of theaters are haunted. How he liked to imagine theater ghosts creeping along those catwalks and watching his plays. So, I told him how we'd met some ghosts—Frank at school and Jeremiah in the library. But I didn't think he believed me!"

"Did you tell him *how* we met Frank

and Jeremiah—about the poems?" Frankinschool asked.

Snake-ula's snakes silenced their hissing to listen.

Princesa nodded again.

"He said that writing was magic—that words and stories made things come to life," Princesa said. "But then he started talking about plays. So I thought he meant that."

"That's why he wanted to come here," Frankinschool said. "Not because he loves you—"

"Hey!" Princesa snapped.

"I mean, not *just* because he loves you," Frankinschool said. "But because he wants to direct a *real* ghost story! With *real* ghosts. That's why he liked my idea so much!"

"We have to find your uncle," Snake-ula said.

"And I bet I know where they are," Frankinschool said. "We need to follow the mail chute."

"We can't fit in *there*," Princesa said.

Frankinschool rolled his eyes. "We have to go where it goes. And I know where that is."

"You mean, we should go *down* the stairs—like I told you in the first place?"

Frankinschool grunted. "Fine. You were right. But we don't have time to argue about that. Follow me."

And all three rushed back toward the twisty staircase and headed down to the lobby.

CHAPTER SEVEN

THE WORST REAR-END EVER

As Frankinschool pushed open a door, even the snakes froze as they all leaned in to hear what sounded like off-key singing and swooshes followed by loud claps and shouts.

"No, no, no!" a voice said. "Try it again… Uh five, six, seven, eight."

"That's my tio!" Princesa said.

"The lobby should be this way," Frankinschool said as they turned a corner and rushed past an empty cafe and small shop. Along the way, the sounds of singing and swooshing and one man clapping grew louder. As did the sounds of arguing.

"You're in my light!" one voice said.

"You sang my line!" another growled.

"You swooshed right through me!" another chirped.

"You are the *worst* camel rear-end in the world!" said yet another.

"Frank!" the three kids said at once.

"And your camel *front* couldn't hold the three wise women even if they—"

"And Jeremiah," they said once again, as they stepped into the two-story hotel lobby that opened to a stained-glass skylight surrounded by balconies.

This lobby was identical to the one Frankinschool had stayed at with his family. Except this one swirled with activity. Above them, ghosts and ghouls of all varieties swooped and swooshed. Some were wrapped in bold-colored streamers that flew behind them like kite strings. Others wore angel costumes or were dressed as stars in the night sky. Below them, ghosts wearing crowns and carrying telescopes twirled across a dance floor with other ghosts in horned, furry Krampus suits. Still other ghosts hoisted candlesticks into the air while still others dressed in velvet capes and top hats stood in small groups and sang carols.

Until they collided into each other, that

is, and their forms melded and merged for a moment before unmelding and unmerging in huffs and puffs.

The snakes stretched and spun and hissed and slithered, trying to follow the action above and in front of them all.

Soon, all the ghosts floated and flew with their fingers pointed or arms akimbo—while accusing each other of ruining their performances and the holidays.

Suddenly, the back end of a camel clomped off in its own direction as Jeremiah emerged, yelling, "I *knew* I should've stayed in the library! Dog gone it! I miss the dogs!"

"Jeremiah?" Frankinschool said.

The back end of the camel stopped, mid-clomp.

As did all the other ghosts. All ghostly arguing ended with not so much as a boo.

A man rose from one of the sofas in the lobby.

"Tio!" Princesa yelled, wanting to run toward him but afraid of running into—literally—the full host of ghosts between them.

"You found us!" Juan Pierre shouted with a whip of his scarf.

"I told you they would!" Frank said, easing himself out of the front end of the camel costume.

"But what on earth took you so long?" Juan Pierre asked.

"What do you mean?" Frankinschool asked. "We had no idea what happened or where you were!"

Juan Pierre pointed toward the balconies above. "The stage was just through that door," he said. "You just had to pop out."

"We went the *other* way," Princesa said, with a stern look to Frankinschool and Snake-ula. "We ended up in the hallways and in the attic with the mail chute and the—"

"Nevermind all that," Frank said, hovering before them. "It's great to see you all again! Or, I should say, it's great for you to see me. I've seen you, of course. What with me living in your school attic."

"Did you steal my notebook?" Frankinschool said. "Did you do all this?"

Frank shrugged. "Not by myself. I had help."

And here the back end of a camel clomped up. "I'd never been in a play," Jeremiah said. "It sounded fun. It hasn't been the case, though. These actors are so *emotional*!"

"You should talk!" Frank said. And he had a point. Jeremiah was a lemur ghost, after all. Famous for their fiery tempers.

The ghosts all began to argue again. They were of no help at all.

Princesa stepped toward her uncle. "Tio, what's going on?"

"I'm directing my dream come true!" Juan Pierre said. "At least I was. A real-life ghost story. With real-life ghosts! I've been dreaming of this since you told me about Frank and Jeremiah. But it turns out trying to mix and appreciate all the traditions and ideas makes people—even ghosts—argue. It *was* a great idea, though—to wonder *'what if all our traditions mixed and mingled and merged and we allowed ourselves to wonder and be a little afraid.'* Isn't that what you wrote?"

"Sort of," Frankinschool said with a sigh.

"Sure, I wanted a ghost story. And I wanted a mix of spooky holiday traditions. But I wanted it to be about the good things that come from all that. How facing the scary stuff helps us in life."

"We did our best," Frank said. "I listened in and copied your ideas best I could. Then Jeremiah fished up your notebook. We got the ideas to the other ghosts as quickly as we could—thanks to that chute."

"But you took my idea before it was finished," Frankinschool said. "Before I let myself imagine the good part of the *What if.* The joyful part of allowing ourselves to wonder about the darkness. You only ended up with the bad part. And now all you have is chaos—all these fighting ghosts."

"Who *are* these ghosts, by the way?" Snake-ula asked.

"My theater ghosts!" Juan Pierre said. "And we do owe you an apology. We didn't mean to steal your idea as much as we had hoped to *surprise* you with a ghost version of your story. You've got real talent, kid! My niece showed me your stuff. You understand the power of pretend and the magic of writing. But we did get it wrong by not waiting awhile."

"My frankincense potion will last another half-hour," Frank said. "Maybe we still have time to get it right?"

All eyes landed on Frankinschool. He nodded. They could all try to save the ghost story play. But the trouble was, Fred still wasn't sure what the point was of his Mixed-Up Winter What-if Wonder Fest. He hadn't written the ending to his idea then—and he didn't have one now.

But then he remembered the ghosts bickering about getting in each other's way. The same way he and his classmates had bickered about whose idea was best and what they should write. The same way friends and families all across the world seemed to bicker about, well, *everything*. Suddenly, Frankinschool realized what facing our fears should mean and what the play could be about.

All he needed was a pen.

CHAPTER EIGHT
WHAT ARE YOU AFRAID OF?

Juan Pierre handed Frankinschool the sheets from his notebook. Frankinschool flipped to the start of his play and reread his words:

> Because fear's what we share, what we have in common.
> Whether we eat turkey or latkes or... ramen...
> What if talking about things that make us shiver,

What if telling ghost stories helps us deliver—

Somewhere up near the stained glass windows, a single voice began to sing: "Walking in a winter wonder fest..." in that creepy, ghostly warbly way they'd heard in the attic.

Frankinschool looked up. It was Jeremiah. Not long ago, Jeremiah had been super scary and screamy. His fiery red face and deep growl had terrified Frankinschool and Snake-ula when they'd gone looking for Princesa in a school visit to the local library.

Princesa and Frank showed them that while Jeremiah *seemed* scary, he was the opposite. He was angry because he'd never had a dog and he had trouble reading and because the town had turned his family home into a library. But getting to *know* Jeremiah—facing that fear—had helped turn part of the library into a dog shelter, where dogs found homes *and* got to help kids learn to read.

That was the good news about fear. Facing it *did* make the world better—or at least, someone's little part of the world.

And everybody was afraid of something. Frankinschool knew that. And as he thought about all the quarreling at the tables and even among these ghosts, Frankinschool realized people argue because people are afraid...of being wrong. Of getting something wrong. Of being different or embarrassed. Of getting hurt or being alone. And arguing over those fears—rather than admitting them—seems easier.

As the other ghosts joined in Jeremiah's rendition of "Walking in a Winter Wonder *Fest*" with *the* Juan Pierre Reyes excitedly standing on a table to conduct this new ghostly choir, Frankinschool realized something important.

"What if," Frankinschool said, "the play is about saying what scares us about the dark, about the world—and then we each light a candle? Together. What if it's a ghost story, told in the dark, about helping each other feel less afraid? *What if* that's the good news of this time of year? That we

find we can lean on each other in times of darkness?"

"Sometimes I'm afraid of how much my moms argue," Princesa said.

One of the ghosts in a wise-woman costume brought forward a candle.

"I'm afraid of bad reviews—and not being able to direct anymore," *the* Juan Pierre said.

"I'm afraid of flying."

"I'm afraid of heights."

"I'm afraid of the dark."

One by one, the ghosts shared what they were afraid of and one-by-one candles began to glow all around.

"I'm afraid of snakes!" Snake-ula said suddenly.

Everyone laughed.

"And I'm afraid of losing my touch," Frankinschool said. "Of not being able to create magic with writing anymore. I'll miss this."

"Ah," Juan Pierre said as he lit a candle for Frankinschool. "The wonderful thing about being a writer or being anyone with an imagination is that you can always create magic. Your friends and the places you long for are always here—in your mind—or here—on the page. You can bring it to life any time you want."

"And we're here to help you remember—and imagine," Princesa said.

"And to be brave," Snake-ula said as the snakes sniped at his ears. "We've been through so much that we don't have to pretend with each other."

Frankinschool smiled. It was true: he could be scared *and* be brave as long as he had his friends with him. Ghosts or otherwise. And being brave together brought laughter in scary moments, light in dark times, and love and hope and peace and joy through it all. The things everyone celebrated this time of year.

That's what was so wonderful about winter—and these holidays. These holy days.

And so, that's what Frankinschool wrote.

> What if talking about things that make us shiver,

> What if telling ghost stories helps us deliver
> A feeling of peace and a sense of wonder
> Whether the days are sunny or full of thunder.
> Because when we tell our friends the things we're afraid of
> We can find peace and hope and joy
> and love.

Frankinschool finished his poem and handed it back to *the* Juan Pierre Reyes.

"I guess the ghost stories in the dark gets us right back to where I started—a bunch of kids holding hands and singing about peace," Frankinschool said.

"I mean, it's not the *worst* idea in the world," Princesa said. "It's actually pretty good."

"Speaking of ideas, friends," Frank said. "Tick-tock. The clock is running out on my potion. Better get back."

Frankinschool thought back over his time since his first poem turned him into Frank-in-school and then Luisa into Princesa Luisa and then Drake into Snake-ula. He thought about the adventures he'd had, the friends he'd made, and the fears he'd faced.

He still didn't fully understand how any of it happened. But that was okay. Because it did happen. Even if only in his imagination.

Frankinschool smiled at his friend Frank. He stepped forward to hug him—to thank him for starting the adventures—but before Frankinschool could, Frank, Jeremiah, and all the ghosts evaporated into the lobby air.

Only a few lighted candles and the camel costume remained.

As Frankinschool turned to look back at Princesa, Snake-ula, and Juan Pierre, the scent of frankincense began to fade and the familiar smell of tater tots, basketballs, and fresh, crisp air began to fill the space. The snakes blew out the candles, and Princesa

snatched up the camel costume as they all raced back up the stairs, through the hallway, and onto the stage.

By the time Frankinschool sat down, he was Fred once again. Fred smiled at his friends and winked back at Juan Pierre. Pen in hand, Fred was ready now to write this play.

EPILOGUE

Dear Fred:

Sorry I vamoosed before the hug. I should probably have mentioned that I hate saying goodbye. Good thing we don't have to.

I'm still around—watching. Does that sound spooky? Ha! It's meant to.

Anyway, The What If Winter Wonder Fest turned out terrific. All those kids dressed as ghosts and spooky creatures singing about peace was perfect. Sorry about the candles tipping over... I whoosh-laughed a little too hard one time.

And, I'm sorry for stealing your notebook, your hotel brochure, and all your ideas. Another library ghost tells me that's called <u>plagiarism</u>. And she said I need to give you credit. So, you'll be happy to note that in the real ghost version that we're all doing in JP's theater (JP, that's what I call Juan Pierre now), your name is listed above mine as playwright. That is, as soon as we can find a ghost to design it for us. These theater ghosts all have trouble with computers. Actors... ugh!

You've never seen as many ghosts in one place as there are here. Ghosts upon ghosts upon ghosts. Some pretty famous faces too. The stories I could tell... When you're older.

Anyway.

Keep writing. Keep pretending. Keep imagining. You have a gift for wondering worlds into existence. And what-if-ing worlds as they should be.

Keep doing that. From my POV, I can tell you: it does make the world better.

Your friend—
Frank

P.S. I know you were wondering about the hallways and candles. I had no idea what they looked like! The brochure only covered the lobby and ballrooms. I thought they turned out great though. Didn't you? I'll have to haunt—I mean, visit—that place sometime soon.

ABOUT THE AUTHOR

Caryn Rivadeneira has spent her life imagining what's up every roped-off twisty staircase, what's behind every creaky, sneaky door, and what's lurking in every spooky space she's ever passed (and it's possible she even snuck into a few of these places!). Caryn is the author of more than 20 books for children and grown-ups, including *Edward and Annie: A Penguin Adventure* (Tommy Nelson) and the award-winning *Helper Hounds* series (Red Chair Press). Caryn lives in the near-west suburbs of Chicago with her husband, three kids, and her rescued pit bulls.

ABOUT THE ILLUSTRATOR

Dani Jones is an artist, writer, children's book illustrator, and comics creator living in New Hampshire. Dani is the illustrator of the *New York Times* bestselling PopularMMOs graphic novel series from HarperCollins and creator of the picture book *Monsters Vs. Kittens* from Stan Lee's Kids Universe.